Playing Wicked

Alex R. Kahler   illustrated by Ben Whitehouse

Albert Whitman & Company
Chicago, Illinois

To my parents, for letting me be who I was meant to be—AK
Twinkle twinkle Timmy and Yvonne—BW

Library of Congress Cataloging-in-Publication data is on file with the publisher.

Text copyright © 2020 by Alex R. Kahler
Illustrations copyright © 2020 by Albert Whitman & Company
Illustrations by Ben Whitehouse
First published in the United States of America in 2020 by Albert Whitman & Company
ISBN 978-0-8075-8739-3 (hardcover)
ISBN 978-1-8075-8740-9 (ebook)

Printed in China
10 9 8 7 6 5 4 3 2 1 WKT 24 23 22 21 20 19

Design by Nina Simoneaux

For more information about Albert Whitman & Company,
visit our website at www.albertwhitman.com.

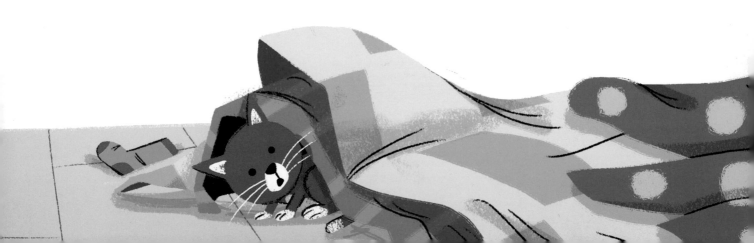

Dante loved playing make-believe.

With his closet of costumes, he could become anything.
A wizened wizard, freezing trolls in blocks of ice.

A brave bard, singing the praises of heroes past.

Regal royalty, ruling with justice and grace.

But Dante didn't always want to be the hero.
Sometimes, he wanted to be…

wicked.

Wicked queens wore the most glamorous gowns,
and cast fearsome spells from magnificent castles.

Alone in his room, he would pick from his favorites:

A cunning queen commanding kingdoms from her stone throne.

An elegant enchantress spinning sorceries with her feral familiar.

A warrior empress scouring the skies on her daring dragon.

Dante had dozens of devilish dresses, but none truly *fit*.
None were ready for the eyes of others.

Until, after weeks of crafting, he had created perfection.
It fit him like magic, all sapphire silk and silver satin—

a water witch in her
gossamer gown,
complete with a crown
of dripping diamonds.

With this gown, he could finally brave the big backyard
and let everyone see his wicked wardrobe.

And oh! The sunlight dazzled his billowing dress!
The wind tousled his long black hair!
He had never felt so wild before.
He'd never felt so *free*.

He rode his diving dragons to kelpie kingdoms and cast his stormy spells.

His armies spread like tidal waves, and magic rained upon his foes.

He was utterly unstoppable!

He could conquer the ficklest of fairies.

He could plunder the titan's treasures.

He could even vanquish the pesky—

prince?

Was Dante under attack?
Should he ready the dragons?
Or was it time to retreat?

Everyone knows a good adventure needs a villain *and* a hero.

Sometimes, we get to be a bit of both.

Dante was not a wicked boy....